# The Monkey Puppet

Written by Leon Rosselson

Illustrated by James de la Rue

# Chapter 1

We stared at him. We didn't get many children coming to the school from outside the village so we were curious. He had blond curly hair and looked too small and thin and young to be in our class. The thing I remember most is that his face was blank. Like a mask.

Mrs Grace stood behind him at the front of the class with her hands on his shoulders. "This is Mark," she said. "He's going to be joining us now so please make him welcome."

A whispery sound rustled round the class. To tell the truth, we resented rather than welcomed new arrivals.

"Mark's new to the village," Mrs Grace went on. "He doesn't have any friends yet so I hope you're all going to make him feel at home."

The whisper became a questioning murmur. Who were his parents? Where were they living? Why had he come to the village? Where had he come from?

I said nothing. I couldn't take my eyes off his face. There was no expression on it. He didn't smile or frown or look embarrassed. He didn't seem to be there at all. I thought he was weird. So I wasn't best pleased when Mrs Grace said he would sit next to me because I was going to be the one to look after him and show him around the school.

Tim moved to another seat so that Mark could sit beside me. He didn't look at me. He sat down, put his bag on the desk and opened it. Then he took out – what do you think? No, not an exercise book or a pen or anything like that. He took out a puppet. That's right, a puppet. A glove puppet with a monkey face. I stared at it, open-mouthed. What was he doing?

I leant over and whispered to him: "You can't play with that in school. It'll be confiscated."

Mark didn't seem to hear me. He put his right hand in the glove puppet and suddenly it came alive. It waved its arms. It opened its mouth. Then it spoke. "It's all right," it said in a funny, high-pitched voice. "I can look after myself."

Of course, I know puppets can't speak. But Mark
had worked the puppet so skilfully, he'd made it seem
so lifelike, that for a moment I really believed it was the
puppet speaking. I hadn't even seen Mark's lips move.

There was a hushed silence. Everyone was staring at
Mark and the monkey puppet and waiting to see what
Mrs Grace would do. I looked at her questioningly.

Mrs Grace forced a smile. "Don't worry," she said to
me in a low voice. "I'll explain later." Then clapping
her hands, she turned to the class and said briskly,
"Come along now, it's time we settled down and did
some work."

I couldn't believe it. Mrs Grace was usually strict. If anyone brought a toy or a sweet or a comic into the class, she'd confiscate it. Now here was this new boy playing with a puppet and she was letting him get away with it. Why? What was so special about him? I was furious with Mrs Grace and with the new boy.

I can't remember much about the rest of the morning. I was boiling inside and my mind was buzzing. I noticed that Mark kept the puppet on his right hand except when he was writing. And since Mrs Grace never asked him a question directly, he didn't get the chance to speak. Twice, though, when Mrs Grace asked the class a question, he called out the answer. Or rather the monkey puppet did in its funny voice. You weren't supposed to do that. Call out, I mean. You were supposed to put your hand up if you knew the answer. But Mrs Grace didn't rebuke him. She just smiled at him, a bit nervously, I thought. I felt confused and troubled and, to tell the truth, a little frightened of this strange boy.

When break time came, Mrs Grace asked me to stay behind. Mark went out into the playground with the other children. The glove puppet, I noticed, was on his right hand.

"I hope he'll be all right," Mrs Grace murmured. Then she sat me down in front of her and looked at me with a serious expression on her face. "You're a good boy, Daniel, a sensible boy," she said. "That's why I asked you to look after Mark."

"He's weird," I said.

"Yes," she said. "He is a little strange. But he's not silly. In fact, he's very bright."

"What's the matter with him then?" I asked. "Why has he got that monkey puppet?"

Mrs Grace sighed. "It's not easy to explain," she said. "But I'll tell you what I know about him so you'll understand better. I'm relying on you to be a friend to him, you see. He'll need you to help him and make sure he doesn't get bullied. Will you do that?"

I don't want to sound conceited but I was beginning to feel quite important. After all, out of the whole school, I was the one who'd been chosen to look after this boy.

"I'll try, Mrs Grace," I said.

Mrs Grace smiled. "I'm sure you will," she said. Then she told me that Mark's mother had died a little while ago and since then Mark had become more and more silent. One day, he stopped speaking. No one could get him to say anything. "Now," she said, "he'll only speak through the puppet. Take that away and he won't say a word."

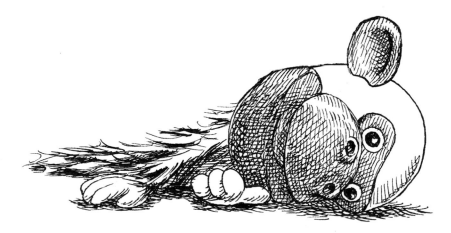

 *Chapter 2*

I understood now why Mrs Grace couldn't confiscate the puppet. But I was disappointed. I'd expected something more terrible than that. Other children in the village had fathers or mothers who'd died or who'd gone away. Poor Elizabeth's parents had both died and she'd had to go and live with her grandparents. But she hadn't stopped speaking.

"After his mother died, he lived with his father and his aunt, his father's sister," Mrs Grace went on. "His father wanted to make a new start. That's why they moved here. They've bought Morton Hall."

That awakened my interest. Morton Hall was a dark gloomy house standing in its own grounds at the top end of the village. We children thought it was a sinister place, especially since the old couple who'd lived there for as long as I could remember had died about a year ago. Since then it had been a ghost house, surrounded by grey stone walls and locked gates. I started to feel sorry for Mark having to live in a place like that.

"His father must be really rich," I said.

11

"Perhaps," Mrs Grace said. "I met him and the boy's aunt when they brought him into school. And I'm afraid I didn't warm to either of them. But there, I shouldn't be saying things like that. I really know nothing about them."

In my head, I was already concocting a fantastic tale of Mark's wicked father and aunt plotting to take over the world when Mrs Grace's voice brought me back to reality.

"What do you think, Daniel?" she asked.

"He's a good ventriloquist, Mark is," I said. "With that monkey puppet."

Mrs Grace laughed. "Yes, he is," she said. "Apparently, the puppet was a present from his mother but he only started playing with it after she died. But what I was really asking was whether you thought you could be a friend to this strange boy."

I shrugged. "I suppose so," I said.

"I hope so," Mrs Grace said. "Now you'd better go and see how he's getting along with the other children."

I found Mark in a corner of the playground, staring at nothingness. He had that look of not being there at all. The puppet was not on his hand.

"Where's your puppet, Mark?" I asked.

I thought maybe, just maybe, he might decide to speak again. He looked at me but said nothing. His face was pale and he had a frightened look as if I'd just caught him doing something naughty.

I looked around the playground. In another corner, a bunch of children were gathered. I ran over to them. The school bully, Pumpkin, was at the centre of the group. I saw that he had the monkey puppet on his hand and was pretending to be a ventriloquist. He seemed pretty hopeless at it to me. I pushed my way through the crowd and stood in front of him. I wasn't as scared of him as I used to be, but he was bigger and stronger than me, so my heart was thumping.

"That's Mark's puppet," I said. "He needs it."

Pumpkin looked at me with that sneer on his face. "What's it got to do with you?" he said.

"I'm supposed to look after him," I said. "He needs the puppet."

"Why's he allowed to bring a puppet to school and we're not?" Pumpkin said.

"He can't speak," I said. "He can't speak except through the puppet."

"What are you talking about?" Pumpkin said.

"It's true," I said. "Mrs Grace told me. He's got special permission to have that puppet. He won't be able to speak if he doesn't have it. He speaks through the puppet."

Pumpkin stared at me as if trying to decide whether I was making it up or not.

"Ask Mrs Grace," I said.

"He's a loony then, isn't he?" Pumpkin said.

I didn't feel like explaining or arguing any more. "Give me the puppet, please, Pumpkin," I said.

My heart was thumping so loudly I thought everyone must be able to hear it. But I wasn't going to give way.

Pumpkin bunched his fist inside the puppet and for a moment I thought he was going to hit me with it. Then Tim intervened.

"Better give him it," Tim said.

Pumpkin looked round at the faces of the children and realised that no one was supporting him.

"I don't want his stupid puppet anyway," he said. Then he threw the puppet on the ground and walked away.

I picked it up, brushed the dust off it and ran back to Mark. "Here's your puppet, Mark," I said.

His face came alive and relaxed into a half-smile. He put the puppet on his hand and said in a voice like Mr Punch, "That's the way to do it."

A shiver ran down my spine. What was I going to do with this weird boy? How was I going to talk to him, to help him? How could I be friends with a boy who never spoke to me in his own voice? What was the matter with him? Why couldn't he speak normally like the other children? He wasn't dumb. If he could speak in the voice of a puppet, he could speak in his own voice. But he wouldn't. He was just being stubborn. He was just being difficult. Perhaps he just wanted to be different. Why did I have to be the one to look after him?

I went to Mrs Grace to ask her to choose someone else.

"Try for a little longer," she said. "Don't let me down."

"I'll never get used to it," I said. "I'll never get used to that stupid monkey puppet."

"You will," she said.

# Chapter 3

And she was right. I suppose you can get used to anything in time. It wasn't long before not only me but all the children in the class, even Pumpkin, were talking to the puppet as if it was alive. Mark was such a good ventriloquist that we almost forgot he was there. It was the monkey puppet that was doing the talking.

It had a personality of its own. It was lively, cheeky, funny. It became the class joker, calling out funny things in lessons to make us laugh.

When Mrs Grace said we were going to learn something about water, the monkey puppet called out, "It's wet," and everyone laughed. And when Mrs Grace brought a pumpkin into the room and asked if we knew what it was, the puppet squeaked out, "It's an elephant," and for some reason we all found that very funny. Even Mrs Grace smiled. She couldn't really do anything else. She couldn't confiscate the puppet and I suppose she didn't want to tell Mark off.

So, to my surprise, Mark didn't get made fun of or mocked, as usually happened to any child who was a bit different.

I realise now why it was that Mark escaped. It was because in a way he wasn't there at all. Or rather, he was hidden, hidden behind the puppet so nobody could get at him. Maybe that was part of the reason he did it. But only part of the reason.

The puppet would never say anything about Mark. I used to walk home with him sometimes and I'd tell him about my family and how I didn't have a father and how my mother was always worrying about me and things like that. Then I'd ask him about his mother and how she died and what it was like living in that gloomy house with his father and aunt but he'd never tell me anything. I mean the puppet wouldn't. Mark would just look blankly away as if he hadn't heard. Or the monkey puppet would squeak out something silly. I often invited him to my house but he wouldn't come. And he never invited me to his house.

That's how it went and that's how it would have gone on, I suppose, if something hadn't happened to change that.

And although what happened seemed terrible at the time, I'm glad now that it did happen because I wouldn't otherwise have discovered the truth about Mark and his monkey puppet. And we would never have become friends – real friends, I mean.

One Monday, a cold wintry day as I remember, Mark didn't come to school. He didn't come the next day either or the next day. We thought he was probably ill. We missed him. Or rather, we missed his cheeky, funny monkey puppet. At the end of the week, Mrs Grace asked me to call in at Morton Hall to see what was the matter. I didn't want to go. I know it's silly to be afraid of a house but there was something about that grey gloomy place that made me shiver. You couldn't imagine children living there, shouting and laughing.

On Saturday morning, I told my mother where I was going – so that if anything happened to me she'd know who to blame – and I set off for Morton Hall.

"Don't be long," she called to me as I was leaving. "And put your winter coat on. It's cold."

"No it's not," I shouted back as I slipped out the door.

But it was. It was freezing, even though a weak watery sun hung low in the sky. I ran shivering all the way up the hill to Morton Hall and stood in front of the iron gates. Then, summoning up all my courage, I pushed open the gate and scrunched my way up the driveway to the front door. I had the feeling that I was being watched even though I could see no sign of life at any of the windows. It was as if the house itself was watching me. There was a bell pull that didn't work so I reached up to the heavy black knocker and hammered twice on the door. The noise echoed through my head as I stood there shivering. Footsteps approached on the other side of the door and I prepared myself to run off if I had to.

But there was nothing frightening about the woman who opened the door.

She was about the same age as my mum, only she was taller and thinner, and her face was hard as if she never smiled. She was, I supposed, Mark's aunt. She looked down at me without speaking.

"Sorry," I said. Why did I feel I had to apologise? Then the words came tumbling out. "I'm a friend of Mark's and Mrs Grace said I should come and see if he was all right."

The woman frowned. "And who are you?" she demanded.

"I'm Daniel," I said. "I'm Mark's friend at school. Mrs Grace sent me – "

"Yes, I heard you the first time," she interrupted. "Mark has been unwell. You can tell your teacher he'll be back at school as soon as he's well enough."

"When will that be?" I asked.

"As soon as he's well enough," she replied firmly, preparing to shut the door.

"Can I see him?" I said.

"Certainly not."

The door closed in my face. I ran back through the gates and down the hill and didn't stop running till I was safe and sound in my own home.

"Silly boy," my mother said when she saw me. "I told you to put your winter coat on."

"Sorry," I said, and went to give her a hug. She was soft and round and warm and I was glad she was my mum.

When I went back to school the next Monday, Mrs Grace said that Mark's father had written a letter to explain that his son had a touch of pneumonia and wouldn't be able to return to school until he was fully recovered. I didn't believe it, I don't know why. Maybe it was the gloomy house or the way Mark's hard-faced aunt had refused to allow me to see him or what Mrs Grace had said about not warming to Mark's father and aunt but I felt something was wrong.

Dark thoughts cobwebbed my mind. I began to imagine terrible things – I'm ashamed to admit what they were – especially when I was alone or drifting off to sleep. Of course, I didn't tell anyone about them. They'd have called me stupid or mad. Terrible things didn't happen in our village. But I couldn't help it. I couldn't brush the dark imaginings away from my mind.

By the end of that week, Mark still hadn't returned to school. On the Friday, as I was going home, I thought I might make a detour, wander up the hill to Morton Hall, just to take a look. What was I expecting to see? I don't know. I didn't have a plan in mind. I certainly wasn't going to knock at the door again and ask to see Mark. It was only that – What? I can't explain why I went. I just did. Things happen like that sometimes without you even wanting them to happen.

So, in the gathering gloom of a cold winter evening, huddled into my heavy winter coat, I walked slowly up the hill to Morton Hall. As I approached the house, I saw that the curtains were drawn and there was a light in one of the downstairs windows. The house has got one eye open, I thought to myself. A car was parked in the driveway. I stood outside the gates wondering what to do, wondering what secrets that dark doomy house was hiding, wondering if I dared creep up to the house to see if I could see anything through the windows. As I stood there wondering and staring, the door of the house opened and I heard the crunch of footsteps on the driveway. I moved away from the gate and flattened myself against the stone wall.

There was the sound of the bolt being drawn back and the gates creaking open. The footsteps crunched back to the house. Without even thinking, I darted inside the gates and onto the grass.

# Chapter 4

This is what I saw as I peered out from behind an overgrown rosebush: a big tall man and a tall thin woman silhouetted against the light from the hall. No sign of Mark. Then the hall light went out. I heard the car engine being switched on and saw the car headlights shoot out their beams into the gloom. The car drove out of the gate and stopped. I saw a figure get out of the car, a giant of a man he seemed to me. Mark's father. He was pulling the gates shut and I started to panic. Supposing he locked the gates. How would I escape from the garden? The walls were too high to climb. Could I climb over the gate? Then the man stopped pulling at the gate, said something to the woman inside the car and walked heavily back to the house.

My brain was racing. He's forgotten something in the house, I remember thinking. He's going to go out with Mark's aunt. They're going to leave Mark all by himself. How could they do that? Where was Mark anyway? A light went on in the hallway. I tiptoed closer to the house, then closer still. The front door was ajar. A light went on in an upstairs room. I felt excited, daring, light-headed. I wasn't at all afraid. I felt as if I was in a film and I was the hero. I was the one chosen to rescue Mark from ... from what?

I didn't know. I only knew I had to rescue him. Without thinking, I darted into the house, saw that a door to the left was open and slipped inside the room. I crouched behind an armchair and waited, not daring to move, hardly daring to breathe. Heavy footsteps descended the stairs. The hall light was switched off. The door slammed. Footsteps on the driveway. A few minutes later, I heard the car being driven away. Then silence.

Gradually I became aware of sounds filling the silence. The sound of my own breathing. The beating of my heart. The crackling of a fire in the grate. I stood up. The fire shed a flickery light into the room. I went over to the window and peeped through the curtains. There was no car, no sign of anyone anywhere. Where was Mark? I had to find him.

My eye caught sight of something familiar, half in, half out of the fire. I went over to get a closer look. Surely, it couldn't be – I used a poker to pull it away from the fire. Most of it was burnt but the head was untouched, just a bit blackened. It was Mark's monkey puppet – or what was left of it.

Suddenly I felt fear in the pit of my stomach. Who could have thrown his puppet into the fire? Why would anyone do that? How would Mark speak without it? I was sure now Mark was in danger.

I rushed over to switch on the light in the room. Then I rushed into the hallway and switched on the light there. Then into the kitchen and all the rooms on the ground floor. The lights blazed out. I didn't care if anyone outside saw them. I just wanted to drive away the darkness.

As I raced from room to room, I called out, "Mark! Mark! Where are you?" even though I knew that, without his puppet, he wouldn't answer. He wasn't anywhere downstairs.

I ran up the stairs to turn on the lights in all the other rooms. One of them was locked. I rattled the door. "Mark! Are you in there?" I called. No sound came from inside the room. Surely he would have made a noise if he was there, even if he didn't speak. He wasn't in his bedroom either. I knew it was his bedroom although there were no posters on the walls, as there were in my bedroom, and no toys either. Just some books, a bed and on the table next to the bed a photograph of a younger Mark with his mother. I picked it up and inspected it. She looked nice, I thought. There was no photograph of his father.

I almost tripped and fell as I raced down the stairs. Mark had to be somewhere in the house. But where? Then, as I stood in the hallway, I heard it. A banging sound. It seemed to be coming from the kitchen. There was a door in there that I'd been in too much of a rush to notice before. Where did it lead to? Someone was banging on the door. I tried to open it but, of course, it was locked. Where was the key?

"Mark!" I called. The banging became more urgent. "I can't open the door. Where's the key?"

The banging stopped. But there was no voice to tell me where the key was. I looked everywhere in the kitchen, in all the cupboards, in all the drawers. I was becoming frantic. What if Mark's father and aunt came back? What was I going to say? They might think that I was a burglar.

Then I saw it. It was hanging on a hook next to the door. How stupid of me not to have seen it before. The key fitted. I unlocked the door and opened it. Steps led down into a cellar. Mark sat hunched on the top step, his head buried in his knees. He was shivering.

"Mark!" I called. "What's the matter? Why have they put you here?"

He stood up and turned towards me. He had that frightened look on his face. He seemed smaller and paler and thinner than ever.

"I'm your friend, Mark. You've got to tell me. You've got to talk."

But Mark said nothing. He just stared at me as if he didn't understand what was happening.

Suddenly I remembered. The monkey puppet. Or what was left of it. I ran to the room where the fire was and picked up the monkey face and the shreds of blackened cloth. My heart sank. It wasn't going to work. It wasn't going to help him speak. There was no monkey puppet now. The monkey puppet was dead.

Mark had followed me into the room. When he saw the remains of the puppet, his eyes lit up and he took it from me. Was he going to try and make it speak? No, he seemed to be searching for something inside the head. His fingers poked as far as they would go, all around the inside of the monkey head. Then, with a half-smile on his face, he drew out something that he'd found there.

"What is it, Mark?"

He held out his hand to show me. It was a ring, a gold ring with red and white stones. He held it up to the light and I saw the stones gleam and sparkle magically.

"It's beautiful," I said. "Whose ring is it?"

But still Mark wouldn't speak. He rushed upstairs with the ring still in his hand. I didn't know what to do. I didn't know what was happening. When he came downstairs again, he was wearing his coat and carrying the photograph I'd seen on his bedside table.

"What's happening, Mark? Where are you going?"

It was stupid. I knew he wasn't going to answer me but still I had to keep asking him questions.

He took hold of my hand and pulled me towards the front door. I opened it and we stepped out into the garden. Then I felt his hand tighten on mine. My heart jumped. The car, headlights on, was drawing up outside the gates. It stopped. Mark's father got out. He seemed bigger and more terrifying than ever. He was pushing open the gates. We were mesmerised. We couldn't move. Now there was no time to hide. He'd seen us. He was walking towards us. We were trapped.

Mark pulled his hand away, took something from his pocket and handed it to me. I stared at it. It was the ring.

"What, Mark? What am I supposed to do with it?"

The figure of Mark's father advanced towards us.

And then it happened. Something changed. That's the way it happens sometimes. Suddenly. Do you know what I mean? Something changes, in a minute, in a second. One minute it's pouring with rain and the next minute there's a rainbow and the sun's shining. Something changes and the world is never the same again. That's what happened then. Mark spoke. Mark found his voice.

"Daniel," Mark's voice said. "Run, Daniel."

It was a quiet musical voice, not at all like the voice of the monkey puppet.

"Run, Daniel!" it said again.

Mark's father was looming over us, staring down at us.

"Run, Daniel!"

I ran, evading the man's outstretched arm.

# Chapter 5

I could have outrun him, I think. I'm a good runner and he was a heavily-built man. So I think I could have outrun him. And then again, everything might have been different. But I didn't get the chance. As I sprinted towards the gates, clutching the ring tightly, I tripped and fell flat on my face. I think I was distracted because I saw the tall thin figure of Mark's aunt climbing out of the car. Whatever the reason, I tripped and fell and scraped my hand, which was still holding on to the ring, and banged my head and dirtied my new winter coat. It was one of the worst moments of my life.

I heard Mark's father's heavy footsteps behind me. Then I was hauled to my feet by the scruff of my neck and turned round. A large, strong hand forced open my fingers and took the ring from me. Then the hand pushed me away.

"Daniel!" a voice called from the darkness. "This way."

I ran towards the voice. Mark took my hand and pulled me towards the gate. We ran out of the gate, past the car, past Mark's aunt.

"Mark!" we heard her call. "Where are you going?"

We ran round and along the outside walls and then Mark stopped and crouched down, wheezing heavily, trying to catch his breath.

"Sorry," I panted. "The ring. I tripped. He's got the ring."

Mark stood up and looked at me sadly.

"Sorry," I said.

"It's not your fault," he said.

We heard the car being driven through the gates to the house. Then heavy footsteps on the driveway and into the road. In the deep silence of the night, every sound seemed to be magnified.

"Mark!" It was the voice of Mark's father, calling from the road.

We flattened ourselves against the wall and looked at each other.

"Mark!" he called again. "Where are you? Come in at once."

Mark shook his head and put his finger to his lips.

"Come in, Mark, we're not going to punish you."

We stood stock still, two frozen shapes against the grey stone wall, hoping he couldn't see or hear us.

"If you don't come in now, Mark, we're going to lock the gates and you'll have to stay out here all night."

The rustle of the wind was the only answer and a silence that seemed to last for ever. Then we heard the sound of the gates being pushed shut and heavy footsteps walking back to the house.

I looked at Mark questioningly.

"If I go back," he said, "they'll lock me in the cellar again."

"But he's your father – " I began.

"He's not my father," Mark said. "He's not my father."

# Chapter 6

Of course, Mark came home with me. And, of course, my mum was frantic with worry because I was late coming home from school. She'd been to the school to look for me and was just about to call the police.

I would probably have been told off except that she was so relieved that I was safe. And then there was Mark and there were the questions and the explanations. I tried to tell her as much as I could but she didn't seem to understand who Mark was and why he was there. But she said he was welcome to stay the night and made a bed up for him in my room and gave us supper and sent us off to bed.

It was as we were lying in bed that night that Mark told me for the first time some of the things that had happened to him. He didn't tell me everything. He wouldn't say much about his mother dying. And he wouldn't say anything about his real father. The man I thought was his father was actually his stepfather. He'd married Mark's mother when Mark was about six. Mark said he'd never liked him.

"I told her I didn't like him and I didn't want her to marry him. She laughed and kissed me and said I'd grow to like him in time. But I never did. When she died, he asked his horrible sister to help look after me."

"Is that when you started talking through the monkey puppet?" I asked.

"I didn't want to talk to them," he said. "I missed my mum. They were horrible to me. They shouted at me and told me off and punished me."

"Why?" I asked.

"They said I did bad things."

"Did you?"

"What if I did? It was their fault. I didn't want to live with them. They said I was spoilt. They said children should be seen and not heard. So I stopped talking to them."

"Why didn't you talk to us?" I asked.

Mark seemed to think for a bit about this. Then he said, "I was afraid."

"What of?"

"In case I got found out."

"What do you mean?"

"In case you found out who I was."

"I don't understand."

"The monkey puppet was funny," Mark said. "I'm not funny. I'm not anything."

I think I understand now what he meant by that. It's like I said before, he was sort of hiding behind the puppet. But at the time I didn't really know what he was talking about.

"What about the ring?" I said. "Whose ring is it?"

"It belonged to my mum," Mark said. "She inherited it from her mum with some other jewellery and some money and the house."

"What house?"

"Morton Hall," Mark said.

"Morton Hall?" I was amazed.

"They never lived in it. They just owned it. When she died, he got everything, the house, the money, me, everything. I wanted the ring because it was beautiful. And it reminded me. But he just laughed and said little boys didn't need rings. So I took it."

"You stole it?"

"It wasn't his. It was hers. She was my mum."

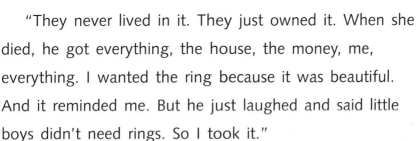

49

"Did they punish you?"

"I didn't care," said Mark, "I wasn't speaking to them. My puppet was speaking for me and he wouldn't tell them where the ring was. They didn't seem to care very much at the beginning. Then he gave up his job and we moved here and I think they spent a lot of money on the house and the furniture, and he said I had to give him the ring. He said it wasn't any use to anyone and he needed it. He said I'd be locked in the cellar till I told them where it was. My puppet told them he didn't know anything about the ring but that just made them angrier. In the end, the puppet said it was in my desk at school. I just wanted them to leave me alone. I didn't think they'd go to the school and see if it was there."

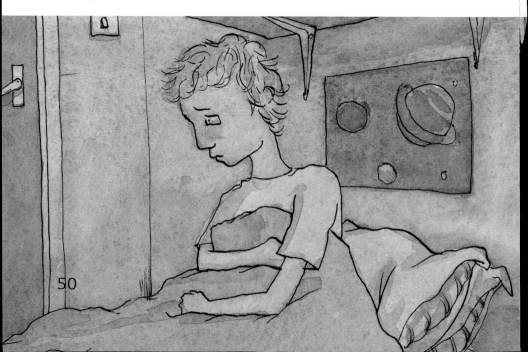

"They never guessed that the puppet had the ring all the time," I said admiringly.

"They're stupid, that's why," Mark said.

"What will they do with the ring now?" I asked.

"Sell it," he said. "They want the money. That's all they want. Money."

"Is it very valuable then?"

"I suppose so," Mark said.

"So," I said, "if you had the ring, you'd be rich."

"I wouldn't sell it," Mark almost shouted. "I'd never sell it."

And then he burst into tears. He just sobbed and sobbed and wouldn't stop. I'd never heard anyone cry so much. I couldn't think of anything to say to him. There was nothing I could say to him. I remember thinking, just before I drifted off to sleep, I remember thinking how lucky I was and how unlucky Mark had been.

Mark stayed. Where else could he go? He wouldn't go back to his stepfather and his stepfather didn't want him anyway. Not long afterwards, we heard that they'd sold Morton Hall and gone away. So Mark stayed. In the end we adopted him. He became part of the family. He became like my brother, like the brother I never had.

Are you wondering if he ever stopped speaking again? No, he didn't. And he never played with a puppet again either, which was a shame because he was such a good ventriloquist. But he said he didn't need puppets any more because he was going to speak in his own voice. The funny thing is that he was completely different from his monkey puppet. The puppet was cheeky and funny. Mark was always polite and very serious. Isn't that strange?

It's strange, too, how things turned out. When I think back, I often ask myself what would have happened if I hadn't gone to Morton Hall that day after school. What would have happened if – ? What if – ? Have you ever asked yourself that question? If you have, you'll know that there'll never be an answer.

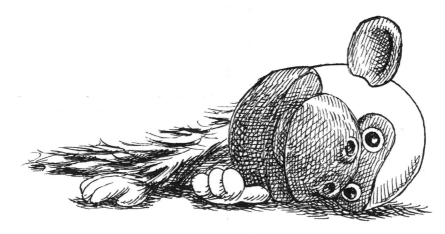

# Story cards

## Event 1

**Setting:** Classroom

**Main characters:** Daniel's classmates, Mark

**Event:** Daniel's class meet Mark who doesn't speak.

## Event 2

**Setting:** Classroom

**Main characters:** Daniel, Mrs Grace

**Event:** Mrs Grace tells Daniel about Mark.

## Event 3

**Setting:** School playground

**Main characters:** Daniel, Mark, Pumpkin

**Event:** Daniel gets Mark's puppet back from Pumpkin.

## Event 4

**Setting:** Classroom

**Main characters:** Daniel's classmates, Mark

**Event:** Mark uses the monkey puppet to make everyone laugh.

## Event 5

**Setting:** School playground

**Main characters:** Mrs Grace, Daniel

**Event:** Mrs Grace asks Daniel to find out why Mark hasn't been to school.

## Event 6

**Setting:** Morton Hall

**Main characters:** Daniel, Mark's aunt

**Event:** Mark's aunt tells Daniel that Mark is unwell.

## Event 7

**Setting:** Daniel's house

**Main characters:** Daniel

**Event:** Daniel worries that something is badly wrong with Mark.

## Event 8

**Setting:** Morton Hall

**Main characters:** Daniel, Mark's father, Mark's aunt

**Event:** Daniel sees Mark's father and aunt leaving Morton Hall.

## Event 9

**Setting:** *Morton Hall*

**Main characters:** *Daniel, Mark*

**Event:** *Daniel finds the burnt monkey puppet, and Mark locked in the cellar.*

## Event 10

**Setting:** *Morton Hall*

**Main characters:** *Mark, Daniel*

**Event:** *Mark retrieves his mother's ring and gives it to Daniel to look after.*

## Event 11

**Setting:** *Morton Hall*

**Main characters:** *Mark, Daniel, Mark's father*

**Event:** *Mark and Daniel try to run away but Mark's father returns.*

## Event 12

**Setting:** *Outside Morton Hall*

**Main characters:** *Daniel, Mark*

**Event:** *Mark speaks first time – Daniel to run.*

## Event 13

**Setting:** *Outside Morton Hall*

**Main characters:** *Daniel, Mark's father*

**Event:** *Mark's father stops Daniel and takes the ring trom him.*

## Event 14

**Setting:** *Outside Morton Hall*

**Main characters:** *Mark, Daniel*

**Event:** *Mark tells Daniel that the man is not his father.*

## Event 15

**Setting:** *Daniel's house*

**Main characters:** *Daniel, Mark, Daniel's mum*

**Event:** *Daniel's mum allows Mark to stay with them.*

## Event 16

**Setting:** *Daniel's house*

**Main characters:** *Daniel's mum, Mark, Daniel*

**Event:** *Daniel's mum adopts Mark who becomes one of the family.*

# Ideas for guided reading

**Learning objectives:** compare different types of narrative texts and identify how they are structured (openings); explore how writers use language for dramatic effects; compare the usefulness of techniques such as visualisation, prediction and empathy in exploring the meaning of texts; reflect on how working in role helps to explore complex issues

**Curriculum links:** Citizenship: Taking part - developing skills of communication and participation, Moving on

**Interest words:** conceited, confiscate, sinister, concocting, ventriloquist, intervened, silhouetted, mesmerised, evading

**Resources:** puppets, whiteboards

## Getting started

*This book can be read over two or more guided reading sessions.*

- Look at the front and back covers together and read the blurb.
- Establish that this is a mystery story. Identify other mystery stories that children know and list some of their features (suspense, spooky settings, unusual characters, etc.).
- Explain that in the story Mark will only speak through his puppet. Ask children to predict why, giving their reasons.

## Reading and responding

- In pairs read chapter 1. Ask children to note the features that the author uses to hold their attention and create suspense.
- Discuss whether the book has a good opening. What effect does the use of the first person narrator have on the reader?
- As a group, list what is known about Mark, and what the readers still want to know.

## Returning to the book

- Ask children to read chapter 2, collecting information about Daniel's character.